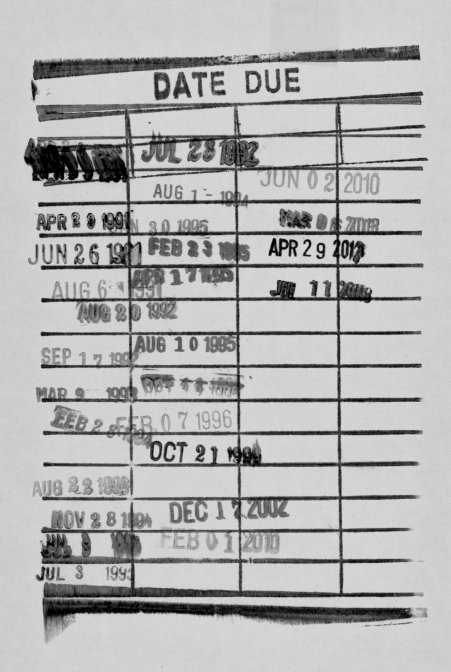

DATE DUE

	JUL 23 1992		
	AUG 1 - 1994	JUN 0 2 2010	
APR 2 9 1991	JUN 30 1995	MAR 0 6 2008	
JUN 26 1991	FEB 23 1995	APR 2 9 2010	
AUG 6 1991	APR 17 1995	JUL 11 2010	
	AUG 2 0 1992		
SEP 1 7 1992	AUG 1 0 1995		
MAR 9 1993	OCT 4 6 1995		
FEB 2 8 1994	FEB 0 7 1996		
	OCT 2 1 1994		
AUG 2 3 1994			
NOV 2 8 1994	DEC 1 7 2002		
JUL 3 1995	FEB 0 1 2010		
JUL 3 1995			

BEAUTY AND THE BEAST

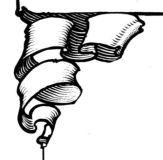
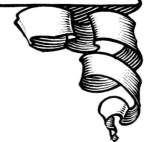

First edition for the United States
published 1988 by Barron's
Educational Series, Inc.

First published 1988 by
Hutchinson Children's Books
An imprint of Century Hutchinson Ltd
London, England

Designed by ACE Limited

All inquiries should be addressed to:
Barron's Educational Series, Inc.
250 Wireless Boulevard
Hauppauge, New York 11788

Library of Congress Catalog Card No. 87-24394

International Standard Book No. 0-8120-5902-6

Library of Congress Cataloging-in-Publication Data
Rudd, Elizabeth.
    Beauty and the beast
    illustrated by Eleanor Vere Boyle; adapted by Elizabeth Rudd. — 1st ed. for the
United States.
    Summary: Through her great capacity to love, a kind and beautiful maid releases a
handsome prince from the spell which has made him an ugly beast.
    [1. Fairy tales. 2. Folklore – France]   I. E. V. B. (Eleanor Vere Boyle), 1825-1916,
ill.   II. Title.
    PZ8.R818Be 1988 [E]
    398.2'1'0944–dc19   87-24394
    ISBN 0-8120-5902-6

Printed in Italy by New Interlitho s.p.a.
890 987654321

BEAUTY AND THE BEAST

ILLUSTRATED BY
ELEANOR VERE BOYLE
ADAPTED BY ELIZABETH RUDD

BARRON'S
NEW YORK

Long ago in a faraway land lived a rich merchant who had three daughters and three sons. The children's mother had died when they were young, leaving them to the care of their father, who spoiled them. The family lived in a beautiful palace with many servants, who attended to their every wish and whim. This was not all for the good. The merchant's sons thought of nothing but hunting and sport, while his eldest daughters became snobbish and arrogant. Only his youngest daughter remained unaffected by the luxury that surrounded them. As the years passed, she was known to everyone as Beauty because, quite simply, that is what she was. She loved the animals, the rivers and lakes, the flowers and the forests of her father's vast estate. She was never happier than when enjoying the simple pleasures of the countryside. Beauty always had a kindly word for the poor and unfortunate, quite unlike her older sisters, who despised poverty. She was, of course, her father's favorite.

Then disaster struck. A messenger arrived at the palace and told of a violent storm off the coast of Africa. The merchant's fleet of ships, fully laden with precious cargo, had been lost at sea. Not one ship nor one brave sailor had survived. The merchant had risked his entire fortune on this expedition — he was ruined. The estate, the servants and horses — all must go. They would have just enough money to buy a country cottage and a few acres of land from which they might scratch a living.

His sons took the harsh news bravely and promised to work in the fields. But his eldest daughters were furious. They cursed their father for his folly and declared that to live in a modest cottage would kill them. Beauty was least troubled by the loss of her comforts but sad to see her father's misery.

Taking with them one horse and a faithful old servant, the family settled down to a peasant way of life. Beauty's father and brothers worked on the land, while she did the housework and tended the vegetable garden. Her sisters spent all their time lamenting their losses.

Many months passed. Then one day news came that one of the merchant's ships had in fact weathered the storm and was heading for port. Hearing this news, the merchant saddled his horse and set off to meet the ship. His two elder daughters made a list of the presents they would expect upon his return. Beauty, though, asked for nothing but some flowers that she loved but could no longer spare time to grow. So the merchant set off on a journey that he hoped would restore his fortunes.

Alas, he was due for a bitter disappointment. True, his ship and precious cargo had arrived safely, but so had all the people to whom he owed money. Wearily he set off for home, not a single penny better off. Tired and hungry, and not knowing how to break the miserable news to his family, he let his horse stray and was soon lost in the depths of the forest. The horse halted in a clearing by a high wall in which stood an open door. It seemed as if he were expected.

He led his horse through the doorway and into the magnificent court-yart of a fine castle. To one side were stables where a warm stall with water and oats awaited his tired horse. But not a soul was in sight. Timidly, he entered the castle by a side entrance.

Burning torches lit his way to a dining hall where, before a blazing log fire, a table was laid for dinner. He called aloud, but no sound could be heard throughout the vast dwelling.

He warmed himself at the fire for a few minutes. When he turned back to the table, he saw to his astonishment that wine was served and a splendid dinner was laid out, ready to be eaten. He waited for someone to appear, but no one did. Famished, he sat down and ate heartily. Then, as if sensing his exhaustion, torches lit his way up a grand staircase to a comfortable bedroom where he laid himself down to sleep.

The following morning, refreshed and anxious to thank his host, he hurried downstairs, but there was so sign of life. He found breakfast waiting and there in the courtyard, groomed and fresh, his horse champed impatiently. Lost in wonder, he took the bridle and led his horse out the way he had entered. Then, turning for a final look at the mysterious castle, he noticed white roses trailing over the wall and remembered Beauty's request. He began to gather a small bunch, glad that he could please at least one of his daughters.

As he did so, he heard a terrible roar and there, before him, loomed a hideous beast. "Villain!" screamed the beast. "You have enjoyed my hospitality, but that is not enough. You must steal my property." The merchant, frightened for his life, sank to his knees.

"Oh no, sir. I am deeply grateful," he cried. "But I could see no one to thank. I meant no harm."

"You presume too much and will answer for it with your life," roared the beast.

"Alas," sobbed the merchant, "I shall never see Beauty again."

"Beauty," growled the beast. "Who is this Beauty? Be quick and explain."

So the merchant told of his misfortune, his journey, and of his youngest daughter whose simple request had led him to trespass. The beast's anger subsided. "I shall spare your life on the condition that your daughter returns here to take your place."

The merchant knew he could never leave his beloved daughter in the care of such a monster, but to pretend to agree would at least allow him to see her again.

"You will be provided with money to pay for your daughter's journey here. But do not attempt to deceive me. Now be gone!" said the beast. And with a bound he disappeared.

Unseen hands had placed a saddlebag across the horse's back. In the left pocket of the bag were gold coins and in the right precious jewels. The merchant's horse quickly found its way through the forest, and within two hours he was home. The elder daughters were all agog when they saw the wealth contained in the saddlebag. Beauty was delighted to see her father safe at home, but she could see that he was troubled. For a while the merchant could not bring himself to spoil his children's high spirits. But finally he could keep the truth from them no longer.

When his sons heard the beast's demand for Beauty they were angry. "We shall find this beast and kill it," they declared.

"Impossible," said their father, "for the beast has many strange powers. You are no match for it. I must return and meet my fate."

Then Beauty spoke. "To go back on your word might anger the beast further and bring disaster on us all. I shall go to the beast as you promised, and perhaps I may reason with him and calm his fury."

The despairing merchant and his sons tried in vain to talk Beauty out of her brave decision. Her sisters pretended to be concerned, moaning and crying false tears. However, they only cared for the jewels and were jealous of the attention given to their younger sister.

In the morning Beauty said goodbye to her weeping father, her sad brothers, and her deceitful sisters. As if guided by magic the horse carried her swiftly to the castle of the beast.

Fearful, but determined to be brave, Beauty entered the castle. It was deserted. At the far end of a magnificent hall was a staircase leading to a door. Trembling, she approached, and the door opened on its own. Beyond it was the most marvelous suite of rooms she had ever seen — a sitting room with frames for needlework and embroidery, paints and canvas to delight any artist, a music room with gold instruments and an ivory piano, a dressing room, whose wardrobe was crammed with beautiful gowns, and a bedroom with a balcony overlooking a fine garden.

She explored every inch of the apartment, finding new delights at every turn. At evening time, a fire was lit in her sitting room and a table was set. A delicious supper was served by invisible servants. When the meal was finished, Beauty heard strange scuffling noises, followed by a loud knock. Her heart leaped to her mouth, but she summoned her courage and in a clear, calm voice called, "Please enter." The beast shuffled in.

Beauty was shocked at his horrifying appearance but tried not to show it.

"Was supper to your liking?" asked the beast in a gruff voice.

"It was the most delicious I have ever eaten," replied Beauty, truthfully.

Although it was difficult to detect any expression on the beast's face, he seemed pleased. Beauty was greatly relieved. He surely cannot intend to harm me, she thought.

"May I sit and talk with you for a while?" asked the beast.

"Of course," replied Beauty, beginning to master her fear. They talked for a while about things of no great importance. Then the beast rose and wished her a good night.

Beauty climbed into her huge silken bed and fell soundly asleep. In her dreams a kindly lady appeared and told her to have no fear, for one day her good nature would be richly rewarded.

The time passed pleasantly enough for Beauty in the castle of the beast. Every evening after dinner he would sit with her and talk. Because Beauty saw no one during the day, she looked forward to his visits. One night while they were sitting together he asked, "Beauty, will you marry me?"

"Beast," said Beauty, "I will not deny that I have grown fond of you, but I could not marry you."

The beast turned away from her, his shoulders hunched. Beauty felt that he was terribly sad. Life at the castle went on. Every evening the beast would inquire if all was to Beauty's satisfaction, and indeed everything was perfect, so she could hardly complain. She did miss her father, though, and asked the beast for news of him. He said that when she was alone she must look into her dressing-table mirror and think hard about what she desired to see. This she did, and she saw her family plainly in the mirror. Her father was well, although miserable, and her brothers had joined the army. Her sisters, with the help of the dowries provided by the beast's wealth, had married.

Thereafter Beauty was more content. Her days were filled with wonderful games, amusements and concerts, all provided by unseen attendants. Eventually she grew quite fond of the beast, no longer paying any heed to his ugliness. They talked and even laughed the night away most merrily. However, always their meetings ended the same way — the beast would confess that he loved her and would ask her to marry him. Beauty would sadly decline, and the beast would say goodnight.

One day, while viewing her magic mirror for news of her family, she saw that her father missed her so terribly that he was becoming ill. She decided to speak to the beast. "Dear Beast," she implored, "I am terribly worried about my father. Would you not in your kindness let me return home for just a week?"

"Beauty, I cannot refuse you anything, but I fear this request," said the beast. "I dread that once you are home you will never return and I shall die of grief. However, it shall be as you wish. Take this ring and wear it when you go to bed tonight. Tomorrow you will find yourself back at your father's home. But after seven days you must return to me, Beauty. I cannot live without you. Do not break your promise."

Beauty went to bed happy that night. When she awoke the following morning she was in her father's cottage. He was overjoyed to see her. Once again the beast had sent magnificent gifts — a trunk full of fine clothes and more gold than Beauty could spend. Her sisters hurried to greet her along with their new husbands. They pretended to be pleased to see her again but were clearly as resentful as ever.

Her sisters' marriages were unhappy. One had married a young man so handsome that his only concern was for himself. The other had married a young man so clever that he spent all his time teasing his wife for her lack of wit.

When the two sisters saw Beauty's wealth and fine clothes and heard that she lived in a castle, her every want attended to, they wept bitter tears of envy. They decided to do Beauty some mischief.

When it was time for her to keep her promise to return, her sisters begged her to stay longer. It was their hope to bring the beast's wrath down on her, so that she would lose everything, even her life. And so Beauty stayed on with her father and sisters. Then, on the ninth night of her visit, Beauty had such a sad dream that she awoke in tears. She dreamed of the beast's garden. There the beast lay, weak, almost dead. At once she realized how much she missed him and, indeed, how much she loved him. Taking from her finger the ring he had given her, she placed it on her bedside table and wished to be by his side.

Instantly she was back in the castle. She ran through the great hall, calling desperately. Then she ran out to the garden, and down to the stream by which the beast lay, motionless. She took some water from the stream and gently bathed his head.

"Beauty," murmured the beast, "you broke your promise. I have missed you so badly, and now I am close to death."

"Oh, Beast," sobbed Beauty, "you must not die. While absent from you I realized I love you dearly and would gladly marry you." Beauty's tears fell on the poor beast as she cradled his head in her arms. And as they fell, the most wonderful change occurred. There in her arms, instead of the beast, was the most handsome prince Beauty had ever seen.

B ut what has become of Beast?" cried the startled Beauty.

"I am that same beast," said the young prince. "Many years ago an evil witch cast a spell on me: that I should take the form of a hideous beast until a girl of great charm and beauty should agree to be my wife. Until you came, Beauty, no one would overlook my ugliness and love me for myself alone. You shall be my bride and, later, my Queen. Never will you lose my love and gratitude."

Now the castle that had once been so silent was alive with music and gaiety. The gracious lady who had comforted Beauty in a dream now appeared and brought Beauty's family to share her happiness. This lady made known her intent to punish Beauty's ill-natured sisters, but Beauty pleaded for them and she relented.

And so Beauty journeyed to the kingdom of the Prince, where they were married and lived ever after in complete happiness.